First published in the United States, Great Britain, Canada, Australia, and New Zealand in 2010
by North-South Books Inc., an imprint of NordSüd Verlag AG, CH-8005 Zürich, Switzerland.
Distributed in the United States by North-South Books Inc., New York 10001.

Library of Congress Cataloging-in-Publication Data is available.
Printed in Germany by Grafisches Centrum Cuno GmbH & Co. KG, 39240 Calbe, April 2010.
ISBN: 978-0-7358-2322-8 (trade edition)
1 3 5 7 9 • 10 8 6 4 2

www.northsouth.com

FSC
Mixed Sources
Product group from well-managed
forests and other controlled sources

Cert no. SGS-COC-007065
www.fsc.org
©1996 Forest Stewardship Council

Helga Bansch

Brava, Mimi!

NorthSouth
New York / London

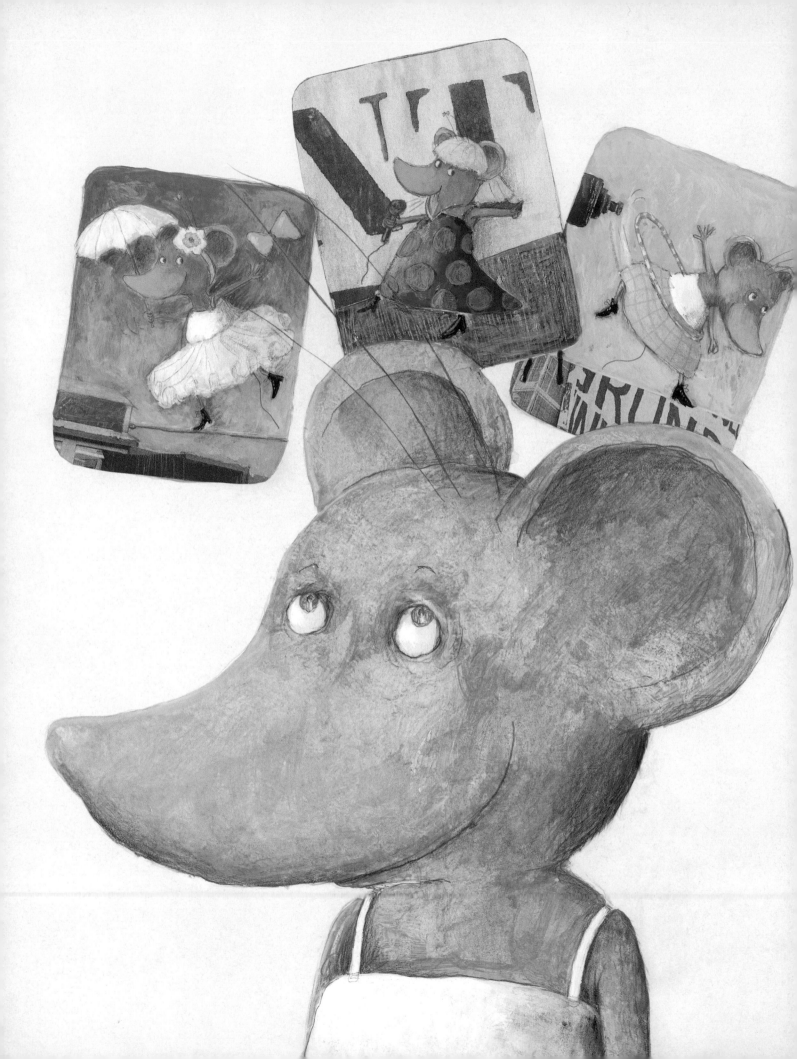

More than anything in the world, Mimi the Mouse
wanted to be on the stage. To sing, to dance, to act
would be wonderful! But to sing, dance, and act,
you had to be talented and beautiful. "And I'm not,"
Mimi thought sadly.

Maybe Albert the Mole could help. He was a reader and very wise.

"You can learn how to sing and dance," he said. "Go to Misha the Frog. He's the best dancer I know."

Misha showed Mimi how to spin and dip and glide. His leaps were almost like flying.

"I'll never be able to leap like you," said Mimi.

"No," said Misha. "You must leap like YOU. And when you fall, always pick yourself back up with a smile!"

Next Mimi went to Bubbles the Blackbird for singing lessons. Bubbles had Mimi sing the scales—up and down, up and down, over and over and over.

"When you sing," said Bubbles, "think of beautiful things. Make each note the most beautiful thing of all."

"But what if I miss a note?" Mimi worried.

"Go right on singing," said Bubbles. "The next note is always the best one."

That night, over a cup of warm milk and honey to soothe her tired throat, Mimi thought about her costume. What would she wear? "You can't practice being beautiful," she thought.

The next morning, Mimi went to Calvin the Tailor.

"We will make you a dress as light and lacy as the finest feathers," Calvin promised. "I will help you."

And when Mimi tried on the dress and looked in the mirror, she felt pretty for the first time ever. REALLY pretty.

"No matter what happens," said Calvin, "you look like a star!"

On the way home, Mimi read a poster that almost made her heart stop.

MOUSE BALLET AUDITION
MUST SING AND DANCE
SATURDAY 9 AM
MOUSE HALL

Mimi's heart started to race. This was her big chance. But Saturday was TOMORROW!

Mimi raced home. She practiced spins and dips and leaps. She sang scales up and down, up and down, up and down. Then she packed her new dress in a suitcase, set the alarm clock, and fell into bed exhausted.

The next morning, Mimi was so nervous, she forgot the way to the bus stop. She had just sat down on her suitcase to cry when her friend Lance the Weasel came whizzing up on his bike.

"Hop on!" he cried when Mimi told him her problem. "I know the way to the bus stop."

But when they got there, they found that the bus had already left.

"Now I'll never get to the audition!" Mimi wailed.

"Don't cry," said a balloon man. He felt so sorry for Mimi, he gave her his biggest balloon. Gently it lifted Mimi up off the ground, and away she floated, right to Mouse Hall.

Mimi joined the dancers waiting to audition. When it was her turn, she remembered all that she had learned. She danced every step and sang every note just as she had been taught. And Mimi was chosen for the ballet.

That night Mimi, in her beautiful dress, was onstage at last. She sang each note. She dipped and turned and spun around. And then . . .

Mimi fell!

The theater went silent. Mimi was horrified.

Then Mimi saw all her friends in the audience. She remembered what they had told her. *The next note is always the best one. . . . No matter what happens, you look like a star. . . . When you fall, always pick yourself back up with a smile.*

Mimi picked herself up with a smile and went right on dancing.

When she finished, the audience leaped to their feet. "BRAVA!" they roared. "BRAVA, MIMI!"

After the performance, Mimi's friends were waiting for her. "You were wonderful!" they told her. "We're so proud of you!"

"I could never have done it without you!" said Mimi. She was so happy, she spun around and leaped in the air. And it was almost like flying.